of co-ordination
is both valuable and
important to a child's later
development, and this is found,
for instance, in *Finger Rhymes*,
the first book of the six book series.

This series provides an enjoyable introduction to poetry, music and dance for every young child. Most books of this type have only a few rhymes for each age group, whereas each book of this series is intended for a particular age group. There is a strong teaching sequence in the selection of rhymes, from the first simple ways of winning the child's interest by toe tapping and palm tickling jingles, through practice in numbers, memory and pronunciation, to combining sound, action and words. For the first time young children can learn rhymes in a sequence that is
r

Contents

LEARNING WITH TRADITIONAL RHYMES

Talking Rhymes

by DOROTHY and JOHN TAYLOR
with illustrations by
MARTIN AITCHISON & BRIAN PRICE THOMAS
and photographs by JOHN MOYES

Ladybird Books Ltd Loughborough 1976

A farmer went trotting upon his grey mare

A farmer went trotting upon his grey mare,
Bumpety, bumpety, bump!
With his daughter behind him so rosy and fair,
Lumpety, lumpety, lump!

A raven cried, 'Croak!'
And they all tumbled down,
Bumpety, bumpety, bump!
The mare broke her knees
And the farmer his crown,
Lumpety, lumpety, lump!

The mischievous raven
Flew laughing away,
Bumpety, bumpety, bump!
And vowed he would serve them
The same the next day,
Lumpety, lumpety, lump!

Three grey geese
in a green field grazing

Three grey geese
    in a green field grazing,
Grey were the geese
    and green was the grazing.

What's in the cupboard?

What's in the cupboard?
Says Mr Hubbard.
A knuckle of veal,
Says Mr Beal.
Is that all?
Says Mr Ball.
And enough too,
Says Mr Glue;
And away they all flew.

8

Robert Rowley
rolled a round roll round

Robert Rowley rolled a round roll round,
A round roll Robert Rowley rolled round;
Where rolled the round roll
Robert Rowley rolled round?

Careful Katie cooked
a crisp and crinkly cabbage

Careful Katie cooked
        a crisp and crinkly cabbage;
Did careful Katie cook
        a crisp and crinkly cabbage?
If careful Katie cooked
        a crisp and crinkly cabbage,
Where's the crisp and crinkly cabbage
        careful Katie cooked?

Anna Elise,
she jumped with surprise

Anna Elise, she jumped with surprise;
The surprise was so quick, it played her a trick;
The trick was so rare, she jumped in a chair;
The chair was so frail, she jumped in a pail;
The pail was so wet, she jumped in a net;
The net was so small, she jumped on the ball;
The ball was so round, she jumped on the ground;
And ever since then she's been turning around.

From Wibbleton to Wobbleton
is fifteen miles

From Wibbleton to Wobbleton is fifteen miles,
From Wobbleton to Wibbleton is fifteen miles,
From Wibbleton to Wobbleton,
From Wobbleton to Wibbleton,
From Wibbleton to Wobbleton is fifteen miles.

My dame hath a lame tame crane

My dame hath a lame tame crane,
My dame hath a crane that is lame.
Pray, gentle Jane, let my dame's lame tame crane
Feed and come home again.

This rhyme can be sung as a 'round'—a piece of music repeated by one or more voices, each entering before the previous voice has finished to produce an overlapping effect.

When the first voice reaches 2 a new voice enters singing the first line. When the latter reaches 2 another voice can enter singing the first line, and so on. The round can then be repeated at will.

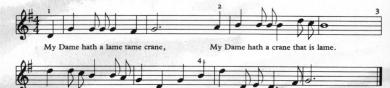

My Dame hath a lame tame crane,   My Dame hath a crane that is lame.

Pray, gentle Jane, let my Dame's lame tame crane Feed and come home a - gain.

17

Betty Botter bought some butter

Betty Botter bought some butter,
But, she said, the butter's bitter;
If I put it in my batter
It will make my batter bitter,
But a bit of better butter,
That would make my batter better.
So she bought a bit of butter
Better than her bitter butter,
And she put it in her batter
And the batter was not bitter.
So 'twas better Betty Botter
Bought a bit of better butter.

I know a house,
and a cold old house

I know a house, and a cold old house,
A cold old house by the sea.
If I were a mouse in that cold old house
What a cold cold mouse I'd be.

Hoddley, poddley, puddle and fogs

Hoddley, poddley, puddle and fogs,
Cats are to marry the poodle dogs;
Cats in blue jackets, and dogs in red hats,
What will become of the mice and rats?

Jeremiah Obadiah

Jeremiah Obadiah
      puff, puff, puff,
When he gives his messages he
      snuffs, snuffs, snuffs,
When he goes to school by day he
      roars, roars, roars,
When he goes to bed at night he
      snores, snores, snores,
When he goes to Christmas treat he
      eats plum-duff,
Jeremiah Obadiah
      puff, puff, puff.

As I was going along, long, long

As I was going along, long, long,
A-singing a comical song, song, song,
The lane that I went was so long, long, long,
And the song that I sung was as long, long, long,
And so I went singing along.

Peter Piper picked a peck of pickled pepper

Peter Piper picked a peck of pickled pepper;
A peck of pickled pepper Peter Piper picked;
If Peter Piper picked a peck of pickled pepper,
Where's the peck of pickled pepper
Peter Piper picked?

Who made the pie?

Who made the pie?
I did.
Who stole the pie?
He did.
Who found the pie?
She did.
Who ate the pie?
You did.
Who cried for the pie?
We all did.

Moses supposes his toeses are roses

Moses supposes his toeses are roses,
But Moses supposes erroneously;
For nobody's toeses are posies of roses
As Moses supposes his toeses to be.

Higglety, pigglety, pop!

Higglety, pigglety, pop!
The dog has eaten the mop;
The pig's in a hurry,
The cat's in a flurry,
Higglety, pigglety, pop!

34

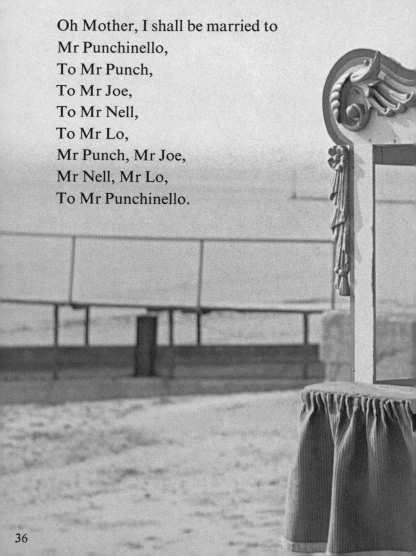

Oh Mother, I shall be married to

Oh Mother, I shall be married to
Mr Punchinello,
To Mr Punch,
To Mr Joe,
To Mr Nell,
To Mr Lo,
Mr Punch, Mr Joe,
Mr Nell, Mr Lo,
To Mr Punchinello.

Round and round the rugged rock

Round and round the rugged rock
The ragged rascal ran.
How many R's are there in THAT?
Now tell me if you can.

Thomas a Tattamus took two T's

Thomas a Tattamus took two T's
To tie two tups to two tall trees.
To frighten the terrible Thomas a Tattamus
Tell me how many T's there are in all that.

Swan swam over the sea

Swan swam over the sea,
Swim, swan, swim!
Swan swam back again,
Well swum swan!

One old Oxford ox opening oysters

One old Oxford ox opening oysters.
Two toads totally tired
   trying to trot to Tisbury.
Three thick thumping tigers
   taking toast for tea.
Four finicky fishermen fishing for finny fish.
Five frippery Frenchmen
   foolishly fishing for frogs.

Six sportsmen shooting snipe.
Seven Severn salmon swallowing shrimps.
Eight eminent Englishmen
eagerly examining Europe.
Nine nimble noblemen nibbling nectarines.
Ten tinkering tinkers
tinkering ten tin tinder-boxes.
Eleven elephants elegantly equipped.
Twelve typographical topographers
typically translating types.

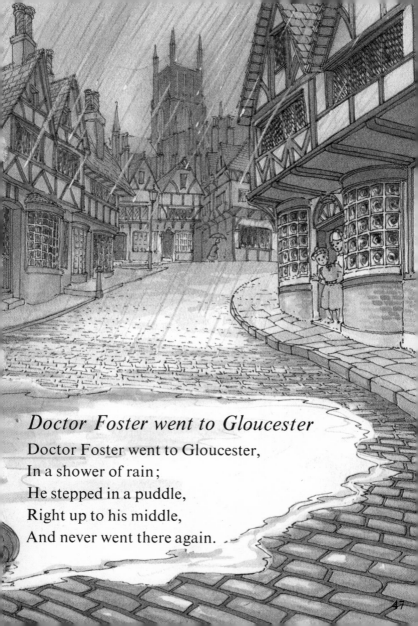

Doctor Foster went to Gloucester

Doctor Foster went to Gloucester,
In a shower of rain;
He stepped in a puddle,
Right up to his middle,
And never went there again.

She sells sea-shells on the sea shore

She sells sea-shells on the sea shore;
The shells that she sells are sea-shells I'm sure.
So if she sells sea-shells on the sea shore,
I'm sure that the shells are sea-shore shells.

The old woman must stand

The old woman must stand
At the tub, tub, tub,
The dirty clothes
To rub, rub, rub;
But when they are clean,
And fit to be seen,
She'll dress like a lady,
And dance on the green.

·❧O❧·

BOOK ONE
❧ *Finger Rhymes* ❧

A selection of finger
counting, face patting, palm
tickling and toe tapping rhymes to
delight the young child and at the
same time exercise his mind and body.

BOOK TWO
❧ *Number Rhymes* ❧

This book brings together many familiar
and some less well known rhymes which
help with the first steps of arithmetic:
adding, subtracting, multiplying and divi-
ding in their simplest forms.

BOOK THREE
❧ *Memory Rhymes* ❧

A diverse collection of rhymes mainly
concerned with days of the week, months
of the year, points of the compass
and letters of the alphabet. With
these a child learns simple
progressions in an amus-
ing and absorbing
manner.